THE GREAT RACE

PAUL GOBLE

ALSO BY PAUL GOBLE

THE GREAT RACE
of the birds and animals

Story and illustrations by PAUL GOBLE

Aladdin Paperbacks

for Bob Verrone

Aladdin Paperbacks. An imprint of Simon & Schuster. Children's Publishing Division. 1230 Avenue of the Americas, New York, NY 10020. Copyright © 1985 by Paul Goble. All rights reserved including the right of reproduction in whole or in part in any form. First Aladdin Paperbacks edition, 1991. Also available in a hardcover edition from Macmillan Books for Young Readers. Manufactured in the United States of America. 5 6 7 8 9 10

REFERENCES: Buechel, Eugene, ed. Paul Manhart, LAKOTA TALES AND TEXTS, pp94–96, 1978; DeMallie, Raymond J., THE SIXTH GRANDFATHER, pp309–10, University of Nebraska Press, Lincoln, 1984; Grinnel, George B., BY CHEYENNE CAMPFIRES, pp252–54, Yale University Press, New Haven, 1926; Powell, Peter J., SWEET MEDICINE, pp476–78, University of Oklahoma Press, Norman, 1960; Stands in Timber, John and Margot Liberty, CHEYENNE MEMORIES, pp22–3, Yale University Press, New Haven, 1967.

Library of Congress Cataloging-in-Publication Data Goble, Paul. The great race of the birds and animals/story and illustrations by Paul Goble.—1st Aladdin Books ed. p.   cm. Includes bibliographical references. Summary: A retelling of the Cheyenne and Sioux myth about the Great Race, a contest called by the Creator to settle the question of whether man or buffalo should have supremacy and thus become the guardians of Creation. ISBN 0-689-71452-1. 1. Dakota Indians – Legends. 2. Cheyenne Indians – Legends. [1.Dakota Indians – Legends. 2. Cheyenne Indians – Legends. 3. Indians of North America – Legends.] I. Title. [E99.D1G62 1991] 398.2'089973 – dc20   90-39983 CIP   AC

The mythologies of the Cheyenne and Sioux, and other peoples who lived on the Great Plains, speak of ancient times when buffaloes had awesome powers, and even ate people. It was by winning the Great Race, in which all the birds and animals ran, that mankind thereafter had power over the buffaloes. It is told that the race was run around the Black Hills, in what is now western South Dakota. From a distance the pine-covered hills seem to rise straight out of the plains, but circling the hills there is a beautiful valley which Indian people call the Race Track. The valley was made by the runners circling the hills, and the earth was stained red with the blood of many runners who died of exhaustion. By winning the Great Race, mankind won power over the buffaloes and all the other animals, and with this power we were also made the guardians of Creation.

BUFFALO
are
DANGEROUS
stay on highway
near your car

Do you know why buffaloes have long hair on their chins?

Long ago, when the world was still quite new, buffaloes
used to eat people. It is true! The hair on their chins is
hair of the people they used to eat. *Ya-a-a-a...* It is terrible
to think about those times...

The Creator saw how people suffered. He heard their prayers for help. There came a day when he told Crow to call all living things together to the hills which rise like an island from the center of the great plains. The people, and buffaloes, and every bird and animal heard Crow calling, and they came to the hills from all directions across the plains.

The Creator stood on the highest hilltop, and spoke to them all: *"Toke.* Is it right that buffaloes eat people? Or should people eat buffaloes instead? All you tribes of four-leggeds and wingeds will decide. There will be a race around these hills. If the buffaloes win the race, they will still eat people. But if the people win the race, they will eat the buffaloes and all four-leggeds instead. Get ready. Choose your fastest runners. Join the side you want to win."

The people chose a young man. He had never lost a race. Even the buffaloes knew he would be hard to beat, but they had a young cow to run for them. She was everyone's favorite, and they were sure she would win.

The animals joined with the buffaloes, because they have four legs. The birds sided with the people, because they have two legs, as we do. Each tribe chose its fastest runner.

Suddenly Wolf and Coyote raised their heads and h-o-w-l-e-d. *Ho po*! The runners sped away with a thunder of feet and a great wind of flying birds.

The birds flew ahead like arrows. Magpie beat her wings fast, and even the tiniest birds left her behind. But she had made up her mind she was going to win. She had been thinking things out, and had made a plan: she flew down and sat on Buffalo's back.

The day was hot. The birds were panting, and when they came to a stream they stopped to drink. But they drank too much, and then fell asleep in the trees. The animals swam past them; except for Beaver, whose legs were too short for such a long race, and he slipped into a lovely pool in the shade of the trees. Otter followed, and Muskrat too.

Buffalo and the young man took the lead, and the larger animals were staying close behind. Magpie had not made a sound; nobody had even noticed her sitting on Buffalo's back.

Jack-rabbit was hopping along well until he saw Coyote
trotting up behind him; he was so frightened that he fled
out onto the plains. He is still there, always wondering who
is behind him.

Nobody remembers how long they raced around the hills; it was several days. Tired runners dropped out all along the way. Prairie Dog wasted his energy chattering at Hawk. Rattlesnake ate Toad and then curled up to sleep. Mouse vanished down a hole when Bear almost stepped on her. Mole and Gopher tunneled along underground, and they still think the race is on.

The young man fell farther and farther behind Buffalo.
He had run his best. Nobody could say he would have run
better. Even Buffalo was almost exhausted, and her head
hung low. Magpie was still clinging to the thick woolly fur
of Buffalo's back. But when Buffalo saw the finishing line,
she ran faster in a final effort. All the four-legged animals
watching from the hillsides cheered her. They were quite
sure she was the winner.

Suddenly Magpie flew up from Buffalo's back. Everyone
had forgotten about her! She was feeling good and was not
tired at all! Magpie flew up towards the sun. And then she
swooped down, squawking and squawking, and crossed the
finishing line just in front of Buffalo. A great shout of
people and birds filled the air.

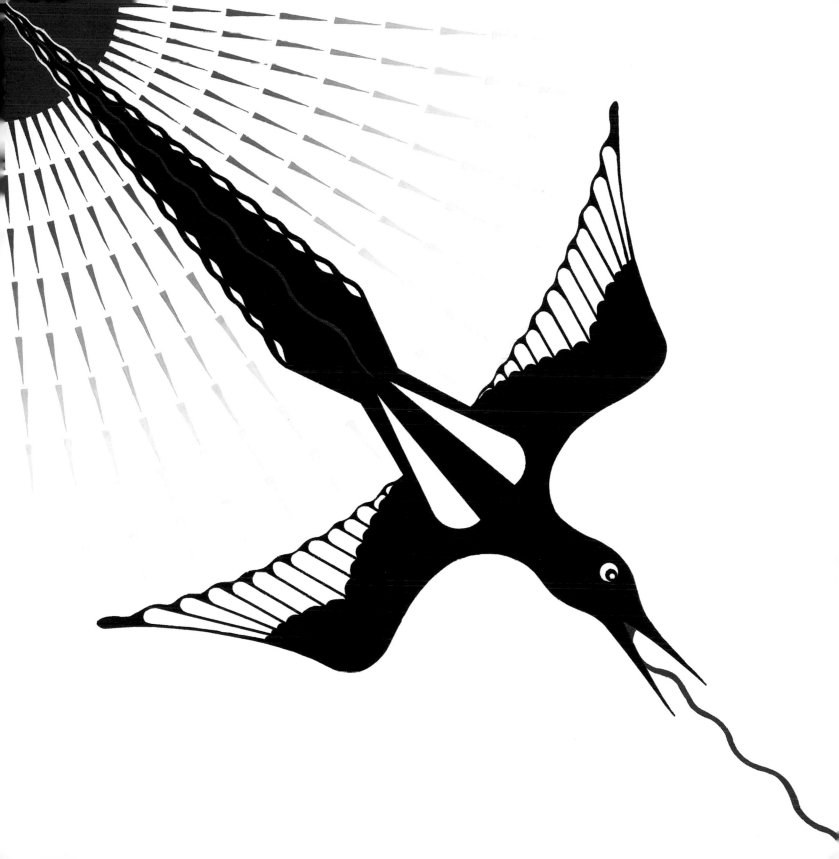

Magpie, the slowest of all the birds, had won the race for the two-leggeds! *Ho hecetu welo.*

The chiefs of the Buffalo Nation told the people: "That was a fair race. Now we are under your power. You will eat us."

And then the Creator spoke to the people: "Use your power wisely. Look after all things that I have made, even the smallest of them. They are all your relatives. Make yourselves worthy of them, and give thanks always."

After that the people were shown how to make bows and arrows, and they were given horses. They hunted the buffaloes when they needed meat.

Nobody ever harms Magpie. The people have always been grateful to the birds for taking their side in *The Great Race*. They honor them when they wear their beautiful feathers.

We can all be a little like the birds: they leave the earth with wings, and we can also leave the world by letting our thoughts rise as high as the birds fly.

It is also told that Magpie flew so near the sun, that the sun's iridescent colors are in her tail—and, in the night sky, what we know as the Milky Way, are the clouds of dust raised by the runners. The Great Race was the start of many things.